Look for More Titles by Cassandra Chandler

LINGERING TOUCH

Gray Card

The Department of Homeworld
Security
Book One
(Second Edition)

Cassandra Chandler

Copyright Page

This book is pure fiction. All characters, places, names, and events are products of the author's imagination or used solely in a fictitious manner. Any resemblance to any people, places, things, or events that have ever existed or will ever exist is entirely coincidental.

Gray Card
The Department of Homeworld Security, Book One (Second Edition)
Copyright © 2015, 2019 by Cassandra Chandler
Print ISBN (Second Edition): 978-1-945702-18-1
Digital ISBN (Second Edition): 978-1-945702-19-8

First eBook edition: October 2015
Second eBook edition: August 2019
First print edition: December 2018
Second print edition: August 2019
10 9 8 7 6 5 4 3 2

cassandra-chandler.com
P.O. Box 91
Mission, Kansas 66201

Dedication

For A.E. Ash—nerdgirl extraordinaire.

Don't miss out on any of the alien action.
Subscribe to Cassandra Chandler's newsletter at
cassandra-chandler.com!

Chapter One

Two things were working at ruining Evelyn's day. First, she was wearing a dress to try to get Adam—the love of her life—to see her as something other than a friend. Second, Adam was having an argument with some jackass.

With irritating sweat trickling down her spine from the relentless summer heat and Adam so obviously upset, she wondered if now was the best time to try to make the leap. She watched him as she debated the wisdom of her decision.

Evelyn had never seen Adam's dark eyebrows furrowed over his perfectly straight nose. She'd never seen his gorgeous eyes—one the blue of the waters off Oahu and the other as green as the immaculate grass in the park behind him—narrowed in anger.

The skin over his jaw held its usual light coat of stubble. She could still clearly see the taut masseter muscle flexing within his cheek. Even his face was toned.

What was she thinking? Blonde-from-a-bottle, too small up top, too big at the hips, her narrow face accented by huge horn-rimmed glasses…

Wait—superheroes sometimes wore big glasses to put people off-guard and conceal their strength. She wore them to remind herself that she was strong too.

Evelyn wasn't going to let herself be cowed by her measurements or society's standards. She was going to go for it. Eventually. As soon as she could get herself to move.

The man Adam had been talking to sauntered off, hands in the pockets of his dark suit. He would probably have a heat stroke any minute, but looked as though he hadn't a care in the world. Unlike Adam.

Adam had his hands on his hips, feet braced far apart as he stared at the sky. His muscular legs couldn't be hidden by the khaki cargo shorts he always wore and his jade green T-shirt seemed barely able to keep itself together over the joy of embracing his broad chest.

Reining in her libido, Evelyn wiped her damp palms on her dress to dry them off, then slid her glasses farther up her nose. This wasn't the time to push the envelope. She could tell him how she felt later. From the looks of it, right now Adam needed a friend. She would be that friend.

She only wished she was in her normal clothes. Jeans and one of the T-shirts she'd made for her gaming group during her undergrad studies would be much more comfortable. She'd been wearing something similar when she first met Adam, plus a sign around her neck that said, "Help! I'm an alien stranded on this primitive planet!" It was her standard costume when she went to comic book conventions.

Adam had actually been concerned when he approached her, and not because he thought she was nuts—like most people. It didn't take long for her to figure out he wasn't local, with all the weird idiosyncrasies in his use of English. Until today, she actually had never seen him speak with anyone else aside from ordering food at a restaurant.

Time to find out how she could help.

The sidewalk baked her feet through her sandals as she approached him. "I'd ask if everything is all right, but it obviously isn't."

Adam closed his eyes and took one last deep breath. "I've had better days."

"You don't look like you're up for a bunch of personal questions, so I just have one. Do you want to talk about it?"

"Not really." He finally looked at her, apparently not registering her dress at all. "I thought we were meeting at your place."

"I know you spend your mornings here. And a lot of afternoons and evenings. I thought I would surprise you. Surprise!"

Evelyn waved her hands in the air briefly. The faintest hint of a smile fluttered across Adam's lips. She decided to build on that.

"Do you want me to go kick that guy's ass? Because I will. I mean he's tall and all, but he's kind of skinny. I think I can take him. Especially if I hide somewhere and pop out at him."

"I have to go." Adam's light voice was barely audible.

"Go where?"

"Home."

"What, like...*home* home?" Evelyn's stomach clenched around the freezer waffles she'd had for breakfast.

Adam had never mentioned having to go back to whatever country he was from. He always said he wanted to focus on the moment and enjoy the time he had. She couldn't believe that time was up.

"When?"

"Three days."

"Three days!" She raised her hands, then slowly lowered them while she let out a deep breath. Bringing her voice to a more conversational volume, she said, "Wow. That's... soon."

"I requested an extension, but it was denied."

"Is that what that guy was telling you?"

"Yes."

"I guess this means the *Planet of the Apes* marathon is off. I can't see you wanting to spend ten of your remaining hours locked up in my apartment watching movies."

"That actually sounds wonderful."

Adam looked so sad. She probably mirrored his expression.

"Maybe we can go for a walk together first?" he asked.

A walk in the summer heat sounded awful, but being

with him, helping him through this and spending every possible second with him overrode any complaints. She tried to smile, but only managed a nod.

"Sure."

They fell in step beside each other, walking close enough that their arms brushed. Adam caught her hand in his and entwined their fingers.

That was weird. He had always been stand-offish physically, only touching her to catch her if she stumbled on a trail or something.

What if this whole time he'd felt the same way about her as she did about him? What if she'd wasted moments they could have spent in each other's arms instead of watching sci-fi movies and eating popcorn on the couch?

If she looked at him she might start to cry, but she was dying to see his expression. She held her gaze steady on the ground. She wouldn't risk letting him see her cry. This was obviously hard enough on him as it was.

Evelyn tried to focus on his closeness. His hand dwarfed hers, his skin surprisingly smooth, given all his rock climbing and other adventurous pastimes. He had somehow persuaded her to come along on a few of them. She was in the best shape of her life thanks to their walks in this park, and they'd only explored a fraction of it. They wouldn't map every inch of it after all.

Her brain practically whirred as she tried to think of some way—any way—that they could have more time together. She wasn't ready for their relationship to be over. She wasn't ready for him to leave.

"You could always put in for another visit, right?" she said.

"No. Where I'm from, they're very strict about where citizens can go. I was amazed they let me come here at all."

"Sounds like a pretty crappy place." Evelyn thought she murmured her sentiment quietly enough that he'd miss it, but his hearing was keener than that.

"I've never thought so before."

Before now, she finished for him. Not out loud, though.

"There are reasons behind the laws." Adam sounded more like he was trying to convince himself than her. "I understand why the limitations are in effect."

"Let me guess. You'd rather not explain them to me." She tried to smirk, to let him know she was joking, but her mouth wouldn't cooperate. It just kept pouring out smart-alecky comments—as usual.

"I'd rather enjoy the time I have left as much as possible. And I'd like to spend it with you."

Evelyn could set her own schedule since the professor supervising her PhD work was gone for the summer. The research journals she was supposed to be going through were piling up from the time she'd been spending with Adam, but she couldn't bring herself to care at the moment. Besides, she'd have plenty of time to catch up on them. As soon as Adam left.

This time, she managed to look up at him and conjure up a full—if fake—smile. "Whatever you want."

Chapter Two

Three days left in paradise. Adam could hardly believe his request for an extension had been denied after his latest successful campaign. Tau Ceti-6 would think twice before launching an attack on neighboring systems again.

Peace was mandatory in the Coalition. Adam's ship was in the vanguard of the fleet that guaranteed it for the septillions of sentients in the Milky Way.

The translation session that prepared him with the knowledge and language he needed to blend in where he would be staying on Earth made his mind provide a direct translation of many idioms. He suppressed a laugh at the quaint naming convention this particularly Earth culture had adopted for the galaxy. They had named it after spilled milk.

He could imagine Evelyn's jokes at his thoughts if she could hear them. *"Better than crying over it. Get it? Spilled milk?"*

Soon, imagining her jokes would be all that was left to him. The thought sent a sharp spike of pain through his chest, surprising him with its intensity. Moons, did he really only have three more days with her?

Holding her hand wasn't enough. He needed her closer.

She didn't protest as he pulled her arm around his back. When he clasped her waist, she rested her hand on his hip.

The years of training for command were barely enough to help him control his body's reaction. Her touch was like fire—as he'd suspected it would be. Her small frame tucked in next to his perfectly. He couldn't help but wonder how well they would fit together in other ways.

Stopping by a small manmade pond near the entrance to the park, he luxuriated in her warmth next to him, the softness of her skin and the firmness of her grip on his side, as if she was trying to keep him with her. The longing that swelled up in him made his chest feel tight, like his heart was filling with a lifetime of memories they could never make together.

A pair of swans paddled lazily across the still water. The white of their feathers struck a stark contrast to the brilliant green grass on the bank behind them.

Adam had seen birds from all over the galaxy on his homeworld, Sadr-4. Always in captivity. Even the Proteus —a bird that shed small fireworks of energy and glowed like a star—couldn't compare to the simple beauty of these swans.

Earth was unspoiled, untouched by the genetic engineers who peddled their wares at all the ports he had visited. Every person he had met in the Coalition was the product of those geneticists. He was one himself—not that they were eager to claim a faulty model as their work, no matter how successful his military career.

"Are you okay?" Evelyn asked.

This wasn't the time for darkness. Evelyn was at his side, her warmth pushing away his memories of cold space. Holding her close, her velvet voice at his ear, he felt a shiver pass through him.

He was far from okay. But he smiled and nodded, looking out over the water.

"It's beautiful here," he said. "I'm going to miss it."

"Don't they have parks where you're from?"

"Not like this." Adam felt her gaze on him and shrugged. "To say they've gone a little crazy urbanizing everything would be more than an understatement."

"Blech. Overdevelopment. It's almost as bad as underdevelopment. I still don't get how you spend so much time camping and stuff."

"You seem to be taking to it well. We've spent much time together in the wilds."

"You know my rule. I have to be able to reach a modern bathroom within ten minutes. That's hardly what I'd call *the wilds.*"

Adam laughed and the tightness in his chest loosened a bit. "I suppose you have a point."

"You didn't have to spend so much time with me." Her voice was low and tight—strain showing through. "You could have been outdoors even more. That is why you came here, right? For the nature?"

"I wouldn't change a thing." He pulled her closer against his side. "You look lovely, by the way."

"Oh, please."

He let his gaze roam over her, drinking everything in. Her hair was walnut brown, but she colored it a pale gold. It was gathered up on the back of her head as usual and held in place with a clip. The rich brown of her eyes reminded him of fertile soil. They were keen and expressive, even behind her glasses.

She was blushing. The paleness of her skin couldn't hide the pink tinge coloring her cheeks and rising up from the low-cut bodice of her pale yellow sun-dress. Her shoulders were bare except for the thinnest of straps holding the garment up.

Much of her back was open to the air. Adam wondered how she had managed to put sunscreen on, knowing how quickly she burned. A surge of jealousy coursed through him as he imagined someone else—anyone else—touching her skin.

"Let's move to the shade."

"Okay."

He led her to a bench near the main path that wound deeper into the park. Ancient oaks stretched their limbs above, sheltering them in cool shadow. He sat next to her—as close as he could.

Moons, he really was losing control.

Visiting Earth had been his reward for thoroughly defeating the Tau Ceti. The High Council hadn't been pleased with Adam's unorthodox request to visit a planet designated as a preservation site, but with it being time for Adam to decide whether to re-enlist, they'd been inclined to comply. Anything to keep Adam at the head of the fleet.

Sitting next to Evelyn with a warm breeze flowing over them, Adam realized they never should have granted his request.

Sadr-4—his entire civilization—had intellectualized their existence to the point that bodies were seen as little more than vessels for their minds. Vessels that were to be modified and crafted to fit the needs of society or the whims of the parents, if they had enough resources.

The society itself was full of distractions——technology keeping everyone's attention occupied, and Coalition regulated cocktails balancing their emotional states. No one seemed to notice that there was anything beyond supplements, technology and genetically crafted skills.

Adam's parents had ordered the political package. They expected him to become a leader, sitting safely in Sadr-4's capital and ordering people around from a desk while they watched on in admiration and enjoyed the status his position would bring them.

"See that man? He's from our DNA."

Well, at least the ability to command had come through.

Everything else had gone wrong. Instead of the color his parents had settled on, he had one green eye, like his mother, and one blue eye, like his father. That was the first sign that the geneticists had lost control.

Adam was much taller than his parents wanted. He towered over most citizens, intimidating rather than inspiring. He lacked the graceful limbs and angular features as well, and his sheer size... There were some ships where he could barely fit through the mechanical tunnels.

He hated to use the word, but he was a glitch.

His parents received a full refund and Adam was transferred from the civilian pod where he had been born to one that specialized in preparing Sadirians for the Coalition's military. From what he'd seen of other citizens, he was better off with the firm but comparatively kind people who trained him—most of whom had similar origins.

Coalition citizens didn't know just how often the reproduction process glitched. The military was primarily composed of unwanted results—people who couldn't quite fit in with societal expectations.

But Adam fit in on Earth. He loved it here.

He wanted to keep breathing air that was processed by trees instead of re-circulators. He longed for the deep laughter brought on by embracing the ridiculous dichotomies of life, and for this—holding someone dear to him close at his side. He had three more days to get his fill, and then he would never be able to return.

"We should get married," Evelyn said.

"What?"

"We should get married."

"That's not something to joke about."

"I'm not joking." She turned to face him, eyes bright and wide. She sat up straighter and leaned toward him with a broad grin on her face. "If we get married, you can stay here as long as you want."

He had a vague understanding of the various laws on her planet about people from different countries marrying, but she couldn't possibly fathom what she would be getting herself into. "I appreciate the offer, but—"

"You're not interested. I get it. My mistake."

She sat back—eyes shuttering, smile gone—and started to turn away. Adam couldn't stop himself from reaching out and gently caressing her cheek, bringing her gaze back to him. The thought of marrying her, of living with her on Earth for the rest of his days... It was tempting.

There were cases where citizens of the Coalition had been assimilated into another culture, but they were extremely rare. Aside from the intense amount of bureaucracy he's would have to navigate, it would mean giving up all of his resources, his rank, even his citizenship.

With his military background, the High Council would probably insist on implanting him with a tracker and a device that would fry anything more sophisticated than a standard computer if he came too close. The Coalition didn't want anyone getting homesick for their technology —or doing worse.

A planet with Earth's technology level could easily be exploited. Adam could pass off rudimentary Coalition tech as his own and make a fortune, then use his knowledge to turn that into political power.

No one would believe he was staying on Earth for love, even *if* that was what Evelyn was offering.

"We can't get married just to fool them into letting me stay," he said.

"Who said it would just be for them?" She tilted up her chin, gaze boring into him. "I have been crazy about you pretty much since we met. I will pass any test they throw at me about why I'm marrying you."

"Evelyn..."

He didn't know what to say. Did she mean she loved him? He hadn't dared to hope, to even consider that possibility. Maybe attraction, perhaps lust, certainly friendship, but love? The way his heart was beating, it was difficult to convince himself that he didn't love her too.

If he stayed, he would have to give up everything...

"Marry me," she said, her voice dropping almost to a whisper.

Adam leaned toward her, not pausing until their lips touched.

Stars above... So soft. So warm.

His tongue slid into her mouth, dormant parts of him awakening with a suddenness that shocked him. Without hesitating for a moment, Evelyn matched his passion. She wrapped her slender arms around his neck, opening her mouth to him and seeking out his tongue with her own. The first touch sent fire flooding through his veins.

She pushed him back on the bench, shifting her dress to straddle him. A throbbing ache built in his groin—his dick went ramrod straight, wanting relief from her so badly he could hardly stand it.

He ran his hands down her back, clenching her hips and rocking her against him. She moaned into his mouth, burrowing her fingers through his hair and crushing her lips to his.

"Excuse me!" A shrill voice cut through his euphoria. "Kids sometimes come to this park, you know!"

Evelyn was first to stop the kiss, sliding back onto the bench next to him. Her eyes widened when she noticed his erection. Then she grinned and draped her skirt over his lap to help cover him.

"Thank you for the reminder," she said. The woman who had broken into their perfect moment glared at them, then turned and stalked down the path. Evelyn called after her, "Have a nice day!"

She broke into laughter, the joyful sound mingling with the wind rustling in the leaves overhead like the most beautiful music. She stood and offered Adam her hand.

"That lady is probably going to call the cops. We should go. That is, if you're *up* for it. See what I did there?"

Normally he would have groaned or sighed at the terrible pun. This time he just laughed along with her, letting her pretend to pull him up. He wrapped his arms around her waist and lifted her from her feet, kissing her again.

He hadn't intended to rekindle the passionate moment they had shared, but the softness of her lips and her inviting mouth overwhelmed his control. By the time he set her back on her feet, they were both panting.

"My place," she said. "Now."

Adam nodded, grabbed her hand and sprinted for the exit from the park.

Chapter Three

Evelyn barely had time to shut the door to her apartment before Adam was all over her again. He lifted her with his hands on her ass, pressing her back against the door and grinding his hips against hers. The stupid skirt of her dress was too long and she couldn't quite manage to get both legs over his waist.

Realizing her difficulty, he reached under her skirt and slid it up to her ribs. He ran his hand along the back of her thigh as he used it to lift her higher. She finally wrapped her legs around him, loving his groan of pleasure as his erection pressed against the thin fabric of her panties.

Dresses suddenly didn't seem that bad.

His kisses were relentless, stealing her breath away. The room was spinning when she caved and tapped his shoulder to signify her need for a break. He reached up and started tapping her shoulder too.

She couldn't keep from giggling. It was a weird moment for his sense of humor to manifest, but that was sort of the way he worked. He leaned back, a dazed expression on his face that thrilled her to her toes.

"I had to come up for air," she said.

"Are you all right?" Adam smoothed her hair away from her face.

"I'm fine. We just might want to slow down a tiny bit."

He used his grip on her leg to pull it away from his waist and gently set her back on her feet. "Of course. I shouldn't have—"

Evelyn slapped her hand over his mouth before he could continue. She'd already figured out that he was the *takes too much responsibility for everything* type, and she wasn't about to let him second-guess taking their relationship to the next level.

"None of this *shouldn't have* crap. I just needed a breather. I have now had it and am ready to resume." She smiled and took his hands in hers, then turned them around and started walking backward toward her bedroom, leading him along. "That shoulder pat thing was pretty funny by the way."

"Right. Funny." He looked a little uncomfortable. Worse —he paused at the threshold to her room. "I don't know if this is a good idea."

"Oh no, no, no. You are not getting out of this."

"Evelyn..."

She squeezed his hands and said, "Why shouldn't we do this? I mean if we really do have limited time... I don't want any regrets."

"Neither do I. I just—" He let out a sigh. "I don't want

to disappoint you."

"Why would you think that's even... Oh."

The idea that someone as gorgeous and masculine as Adam could have performance problems was beyond ironic, but it was the only thing that came to mind when trying to think of how he might disappoint her.

She wrapped her arms around his shoulders and pulled herself up on her tip-toes to nibble his earlobe. He groaned and put his hands on her waist. That was progress. Now if she could just get him into her bedroom.

"You don't have to worry about that with me," she said. "Besides if things don't go exactly as we hope, there are lots of other things we can do."

"What kinds of things?"

"Are you looking for dirty talk? I'm not sure how good I am at that, but I'll give it a try if you want."

"No, I..." He lowered his head to her shoulder. "I think I should go."

"What?"

Her stomach started to churn. She gripped his shoulders and pushed him far enough away that she could see his expression and try to figure out what was going on.

His lips were slightly parted, eyes still unfocused, and he seemed a little unsteady on his feet. Maybe he wasn't feeling that stable himself. He lifted a hand as if to touch her cheek, then winced and curled his fingers into a fist before lowering his arm back to his side. Resolve was seeping into his expression and Evelyn had a feeling she was not going to be pleased with his decision.

"Do you want to go?" She did her best to hide her own desire, her desperate longing for him to stay, whether they had sex or not.

Adam stared at her for what felt like a long time. "This is more complicated than you think."

She was tempted to say something about their body parts and inserting tab A into slot B to break the tension, but she resisted.

"Help me understand," she said.

"We have different customs where I'm from. We do things...differently."

How different could it be? Evelyn shrugged. "I'm open to trying new things."

"We aren't. I mean, *I* am. But where I'm from... We keep things simple. This is already much more than what I've experienced before."

The ground seemed to shift beneath her. All they'd done so far was kiss. Sure, they were the best kisses she'd ever had and that bit against the door was fabulous, but they hadn't even passed second base.

"Wait, you're not telling me you're a virgin, are you?" she asked.

"No, of course not. I've just never experienced anything this intense."

She tried to make sense of what he was saying. He'd had

sex before, but hadn't done anything as intense as their make-out session.

Well, that took all the pressure off. If Adam wound up leaving, she'd make sure he had some amazing memories to take with him. Hell, maybe she could convince him to marry her just for the sex.

"So, you've had sex, but it's always been boring?"

He let out a laugh and his shoulders lowered a bit. "That is a good way of putting it."

"Oh, I will show you a good way to put it." She cringed. "That sounded better in my head. I did say I'm not good at dirty talk."

"I'm not going to be able to tell. I thought you patting my shoulder was some kind of move."

Laughing, she said, "Then why don't you let me show you some real moves? Just promise to tell me if you object to anything."

"I don't see that happening, but I promise."

"Boring sex, huh?" She wrapped her arms around his neck. "You are *so* going to marry me."

Before he could say anything else, she kissed him. He let her lead this time and she kept it light and slow. For the moment. She walked backward into her room, keeping her grip on his neck and her lips on his. She didn't want him having any more second thoughts.

She guided him carefully to her bed, avoiding the model planets, stars, and spaceships she had painted and hung from her ceiling that were low enough to hit his head. She'd have to do something about that later. He was taller than she'd thought, and she hoped this wouldn't be the first and last time he was in her bedroom.

When they reached the bed, she let her hands drop to his stomach, tracing the muscles she'd suspected were there. She pulled up his shirt, dragging it over his head and throwing it on the floor.

"Holy crap!" Evelyn couldn't stop her outburst.

She gaped at his perfect pectorals coated in fine dark hair, the lines of sinew and muscle cording his shoulders and arms, the rows of abdominal muscles standing at attention in orderly rows down his stomach, the two graceful divots marking the iliac crest of his pelvis…

A brief moment of self-doubt sparked within her. Adam could have any woman he wanted.

Evelyn brought out her mental fire extinguisher. He wanted *her*.

He was brilliant. She knew that because he was one of the few people she'd met who could keep up with the vagaries of her mind. He had to be most enamored with her intellect and personality, based on the vast discrepancy between their physiques. Which made it all the worse that he was leaving.

Sadness was just as unwelcome as self-doubt. And she had promised Adam—and herself—a good time.

"Is something wrong?" he asked.

"No. Absolutely not." She grinned at the terrible joke. Always falling back on humor. "Get it? *Abs*olutely?"

Adam raised an eyebrow.

"Sorry. I can't help myself. And this—" she gestured at his chest "—is so magnificent. It's a little intimidating, with me and my three-bags of chips a week habit and Internet addiction."

"I think you're beautiful."

"I bet you say that to all the women who promise you the best sex of your life."

"I've only ever said it to you."

Evelyn's brain just stopped. Jokes, thoughts, plans—they all evaporated. He ran a finger over her ear, pushing a stray lock of hair away from her face. He stared at every feature, as if he was trying to memorize her. She actually... believed him.

Her body kicked in as her brain bowed out. *Want. Need.* She would show him that he belonged with her, letting her body lead the way.

Chapter Four

Thinking about his home world cooled his ardor somewhat until Evelyn kissed him again. Adam let himself sink into the sensation of her lips against his, her cool fingers on his chest—exploring, teasing. Her hands were bold, hungry, unlike anything he'd ever experienced before. There was so much need behind her touch.

Feather-light, she dusted the backs of her fingers against his navel, trailing them over the smooth skin of his stomach to the fastener of his shorts. She worked the button deftly, opening them just enough to reach in and stroke him through the soft cotton of his underwear.

He drew in a breath like he was surfacing from an ocean. Without using *Coupling*, the drug the Coalition provided citizens to meet their sexual needs or facilitate sex with a partner, even that touch made lightning arcs of pleasure streak through him. He was used to stimulation coming from chemicals flooding his body, not from his actual senses.

He could feel her smile against his lips.

Turning her lips to his ear, she gently raked her teeth

over his jaw. "Tell me your lovers at least touched you here."

"Not like this." He was surprised he could get out the words. His chest felt tight, his entire body filled to the brim with feelings that threatened to shatter him at any moment.

She sank to her knees before him, then quickly untied the laces of his boots, helping him out of them. His socks joined the pile of discarded clothing, along with his shorts. She slowed as she pulled his boxer-briefs down his legs, her breath hitching as she stared at his erection.

When he was completely naked, she looked up at him with a wicked smile.

"Did they touch you like this?" she said.

He wasn't sure what she meant. Before he could ask, she licked the crown of his dick.

His entire body jerked in response to the intense pleasure that reverberated out from his groin. She kept her gaze locked on his, that smile curving her lush mouth as she took another long lick from the base of his shaft to the crown.

"Cygnus X! What are you doing?"

"Making you have nerdy outbursts, apparently." She ran her cheek down the length of him, practically purring.

"What?"Adam forgot for a moment what they were talking about. All he knew was that he wanted more.

"Cygnus X?" she said.

Moons, how could he have made such an error? His

translation session changed almost all of his vocabulary to match that of Earth, even in their naming of things, but exclamations of that sort seemed outside of the mental programming. Evelyn had taught him quite a few slang terms and epithets, but he didn't realize his own had been translated into her language. At least he could explain it away with relative ease.

"I must have read it somewhere," he said.

This was too dangerous. He had to stop. He reached toward her to pull her away, but when his fingers touched her silken hair, he found himself instead taking out the clip and casting it away. All that honey-gold spilled around him, framing her face as she smiled up at him. Then she parted her lips and took him into her mouth.

"Evelyn!"

She circled her hands around him again, her eyes finally lowering to his dick. "Wow, you are huge. I'm going to need quite a warm-up to accommodate you."

A warm-up after this? Adam's skin was on fire, his muscles writhing with need—to hold her, to push himself into her over and over until oblivion claimed them both.

But she had been seeing to his pleasure. Moons, how she'd been doing so. He wasn't sure how to reciprocate. What she was doing to him was primal.

"Tell me what to do," he rasped.

"I do like a man who can take orders."

If only she knew. Adam commanded starships. He was

used to being the one who gave orders, and he was used to being obeyed. But in her hands, in her mouth, he found he would do anything to please her, anything to stay with her.

The thought was natural, the decision effortless. He was only surprised it had taken him so long to realize how strong his feelings for her had become. Beyond the amazing things she was doing to his body—her humor, her wit, her spirit, were all things he couldn't live without.

Exist, yes. Live? No.

"Have a seat," she said. She leaned back from him and stood, then bent to take off her sandals.

Adam sat on the bed. He couldn't keep from staring at her, wondering what was next. He was always wondering that with her. He never knew what she would say or do. It was what made their time together so magical, part of why he loved her.

How could he have not realized that? He *loved* her. Absolutely. And that was why giving up everything to be with her wouldn't be a sacrifice at all. It was a necessity.

The realization snapped what was left of his self control. He gripped her waist, pulling her onto his lap. He crushed his mouth to hers, his tongue delving, exploring.

She moaned against his lips, pressing herself against his erection. He slid his hands up her back, finding the zipper for her dress and making quick work of it. The warmth of her skin called to him, but he wanted more.

Flipping her over onto the bed, he pulled her dress down

her body and cast it away. He slid her panties down her legs, letting his fingers delight in the warmth of her skin, the fullness of her thighs. Her body was decadently feminine.

"This seems like the point where I should tell you I have a birth control implant," Evelyn said. "I'm not that active and have been tested recently for...unpleasantness. I'm all good. You?"

Cygnus X, how could he have not thought of something so important?

He swallowed hard, his dick pulsing as he stared at her. Nothing had ever affected him as Evelyn did.

"I was rigorously tested before coming here to be sure I wasn't carrying anything harmful," he said.

"Awesome. Well, now that we have that out of the way..." She reached for him, drawing him down to lay beside her.

So much warmth. He pressed his chest to hers as he kissed her again, marveling at the softness of her skin.

She had mentioned concern about them coupling. Her body needed to be prepared for him naturally. Perhaps it would be best to start smaller.

He cupped her sex, then slowly slid his finger into her core, amazed at the different textures, the sensation of her body inviting him in. He had never touched a woman this intimately with his hands.

"More. Adam, more."

She couldn't be ready for him yet. He slid another finger into her, never pausing in his movements.

"Oh God, yes!"

His dick was so hard. It throbbed with need, longing to fill her. But he wanted her to enjoy their coupling as much as he was certain to. A third finger joined the others, her body clenching them tight.

"Wait, wait! Stop!"

Adam quickly pulled back, wondering if he'd hurt her or offended her somehow. She was panting, one hand on her forehead.

"That's enough. I'm ready."

Those were the most beautiful words he'd ever heard. He didn't trust himself to speak, to think, to do anything except press her back into the bed, his shaft finding its perfect place immediately.

Soft. Hot. Wet.

He wanted to go slowly, but once he touched himself to her, it was over. He buried himself deep, crying out from the intense sensations scattering through him. His body was a live conduit, sparking from the overload to his senses.

He wanted to be deeper, he wanted to feel more, to give her more. Gripping her thighs, he pulled her legs up to rest on the bed, holding them in place against his arms. The angle gave him more—just a little more—but he would take whatever he could get, whatever she would give him.

She gripped his neck, holding on as he rocked her

against the bed. Her eyes were clenched shut, mouth open as she gasped for breath.

Her back arched, head thrashing as her hips bucked against his. He kept going, pumping into her, barely controlling himself as he felt her body coil around his, the rhythmic contractions pulling on him, urging him to give in to his own climax.

It lit like a fuse from where they were joined. The flame traveled up his body, through his chest, down his legs and arms, consuming his mind, his memory of anything before her, before *this*. He screamed with the pureness of it, as all that he had been before was burned away. Still thrumming, chest heaving for breath, he collapsed on top of her on the bed.

She was his. She would always be his. His body still wanted to move within her, on top of her, but he was too relaxed—more than he had ever been.

He didn't know how much time passed before she said, "Um, getting a little difficult to breathe down here."

"My apologies."

She laughed as he rolled over onto his back, which reassured him that she was all right. Evelyn propped herself up on her elbows and grinned at him, her full lips pulled in a devastating smile. Her face was still flushed, eyes bright, hair a glorious halo of gold around her soft features.

"You are so beautiful," he said.

"Eh, you probably say that to all the women who let you

fuck them senseless."

He laughed again, deeper and longer than he ever had. His chest felt spacious, like shackles that he hadn't known he wore had been cast off.

He felt infinite.

This couldn't end. Ever. He stood and helped her to sit up, then knelt in front of her again.

Adam took one of her hands in both of his. He couldn't stop smiling. "I'm not going to marry you because I want to stay here. I'm not going to marry you because of what just happened, even though it was truly the most amazing experience of my life."

One corner of her lips pulled into a knowing smirk. "But you *are* going to marry me."

"Yes. Because I love you."

Chapter Five

Had she just heard him correctly? Love?

Evelyn's heart was too small to hold all the emotions she was feeling. It seemed to split in two. One half pounded frantically in her chest and the other lodged itself soundly in her throat.

"Marry me," he said.

Adam's smile was gentle, even though what they had just done really kind of wasn't. She'd suspected he would be passionate in bed if she could convince him to let go of some of that self-control, but...

Wait, what did he just say?

"Evelyn. Marry me."

Her brain didn't seem to be working, but luckily her mouth was doing fine. "Okay."

His smile brightened and he rose up on his knees to kiss her again, hands cradling her face. The kiss was gentle and slow, as if they had all the time in the world. Maybe now they actually did.

"I have to go."

She shook her head to clear it. That didn't seem right.

"Great. Because that's what every woman wants to hear after a declaration of love, mind blowing sex and a proposal."

"I only have two and a half days left. If I don't get everything in order, I'll have to leave no matter what."

"Well then, why are you kneeling naked in my bedroom? Go!"

She waved her hands at him to shoo him on his way, but he caught her by her wrists, then pulled her against his chest and wrapped her arms around his neck. She laughed as she fell into him, still exhilarated from everything that had happened.

He kissed her again, one of those mind-numbing, earth-shattering kisses. She could feel his erection poking her thigh and wondered if she might be able to convince him to stay a little bit longer.

"Are you sure you don't have another fifteen minutes? I can teach you about this thing we call a *quickie*."

Adam chuckled deep in his chest. He nuzzled her neck and said, "You make it sound tempting, but I really do need to go. There's much to do to make sure everything is in order."

He stepped away from her and started to gather up his clothes.

"Far be it from me to disagree with my fiancé." She still couldn't believe it. Fiancé? Was she really engaged?

"I hope you do keep disagreeing with me. And making

me laugh and surprising me at every turn."

"I'll do my best, but it might be *hard* to keep that *up*." She giggled. "Get it?"

"I'll *pun*ish you for that later."

She couldn't believe he'd made such a terrible joke. Sure, she usually earned a laugh when she made them, but the fact that he'd loosened up enough to make bad jokes of his own...

Evelyn threw herself back on her bed, covering her face with her hands. "Oh my God, you're perfect."

"The student becomes the master. You did teach me all about puns."

She laughed, then rolled off her bed and headed for her dresser. Adam had already managed to get dressed and was tying his boots.

"What are you doing?"

"Getting dressed." She pulled on a pair of jeans and grabbed her favorite T-shirt—a 50s style flying saucer hovering over the words, *I believe*. With the shirt halfway over her head, she said, "I don't know if you picked up on this over the last couple of months, but I don't usually sit around my apartment naked."

"I'll have to fix that." He grinned at her, tugging her shirt down the rest of the way.

"Oh, I look forward to that. But in the meantime, since you're going to be gone for a while and we'll probably be pretty busy when you get back," she waggled her eyebrows, "I'm going to see what I can get done at the University. Meet you here tonight?"

"I'll be back as soon as I can, but I don't know how long it will be."

She slid her hands up his chest. She would never get tired of feeling him, touching him, being close to him. She wrapped her arms around his neck and pulled herself up so that their noses were touching.

"Then give me a little sugar to tide me over," she said.

"You are ridiculous."

"You are not kissing me."

"I'll have to fix that too."

"They better let you stay," she said. "You have a lot to do."

He kissed her then—soundly, deeply. The model planets above their heads seemed to spin as his lips caressed hers, his tongue stoking the fire in her belly yet again. Evelyn used what willpower she had left to push him away.

"If you don't leave now, I'm going to tie you to the bed and keep you here until I'm well and truly done with you," she said.

"Done with me?"

"That was a poor choice of words. I don't think I'll ever be done with you."

"Good. Because I know I'll never be done with you."

She walked him to the door, holding hands the whole way. She felt giddy, so excited at the new prospects before her that she hardly knew what to think.

At the door, Adam said, "That thing you mentioned about tying me to the bed... Do people really do that?"

Evelyn grinned. "Later."

He kissed her once more before he left. A lingering kiss, his gaze promising more. She could hardly wait until tonight. But in the meantime, there were some research journals that she could bury herself in that might help her pass the time.

Chapter Six

"I'm staying."

Adam burst through the door to the planetary liaison's office, a little gratified that his entrance made Todd jump behind the heavy wooden desk that dominated the large room. Adam planted his feet on the ground, daring Todd to object.

Something was wrong. Instead of being cowed, Todd leaned back in his chair and smirked. He draped one of his arms across the surface of his desk and kept the other out of sight beneath it. From the angle of his elbow, his hand wasn't resting in his lap.

Amateur. Todd was broadcasting the weapon he had strapped to the underside of the desk. Why he had a weapon pointed at his door was the mystery. Without seeing it, Adam couldn't tell the range or dispersal pattern he was facing.

"I've told you the High Council's decision," Todd said. "You'll have to take it up with them. In person."

Adam stalked to a low table along the left wall of the room, hopefully out of the path of whatever Todd was hiding beneath his desk. Turning, Adam leaned against the table, crossing his arms.

"Actually, *you'll* be taking it up with them," Adam said. "I'm done with the Coalition."

"You can't just quit the Coalition."

"My latest tour is complete. My obligations are fulfilled. I'm officially releasing my citizenship so that I can stay on Earth."

Todd stood and smoothed the jacket of his suit—dark fabric made of native materials of extremely high quality. He walked around the desk and leaned against it, mirroring Adam's posture.

"I know it's nice here, but you can't just stay. It was enough of a stretch that you were allowed to come here in the first place. This is precisely why Earth is a preserved planet. There are too many temptations here for someone like you."

"What, you mean a glitch?"

Todd's lips flickered into a sneer for the briefest of moments, but Adam caught the expression. Todd recovered himself quickly.

"A conqueror," Todd said.

Adam couldn't argue that point. "Not anymore."

"Really? You can guarantee to the High Council that you won't snatch up some choice technology when you get bored with all your nature hikes, cobble it together into something that actually works, and bring these primitive people to their knees?"

An image of Evelyn before Adam on her knees sprang to mind. He had to clamp down on his body's reaction with all his willpower to keep himself from getting hard just from the thought. When he looked back at Todd, the bastard had a smug smirk on his face.

"I see. You've tasted even more of the forbidden fruits of this planet than I thought. The women here do have their charms. I have yet to find one immune to my own."

Adam couldn't believe that the planetary liaison had taken such liberties with the people he was supposed to be protecting. Adam kept his expression as impassive as he could, seething inside.

Todd shook his head and walked back to his chair, but didn't sit. "My advice is to find a few Earth women to teach you their tricks and then hire someone on one of the stations to service your new appetites when you get back."

Adam had made a dangerous assumption about Todd—and was paying for it. Being assigned to Earth was an important role for a planetary liaison. They were supposed to be carefully screened. They were also supposed to protect the populace of the planet they were overseeing, not offer them up as entertainment.

"I'm only interested in one woman," Adam said. "And she's on Earth, so that's where I'm staying. Draw up whatever forms you need. Citizen revocation, contracts of conduct, relinquishing my assets."

A spark lit in Todd's eyes at the last. Adam was hardly surprised. Apparently, Todd had been on Earth long enough to be corrupted by the vast resources of the planet. He masked his expression, most likely realizing that he wasn't being as discreet as he needed to be.

"You can't just buy yourself a spot on this planet." Todd sat again, leaning back and steepling his fingers, elbows on the arms of his chair. "If people could, the place would be overrun. Half the planets with preservation status would be."

"I'm not some tourist looking for a permanent vacation. I don't make these choices lightly."

Todd was silent for a while. The unwholesome gleam in his eyes caused Adam's stomach to clench.

Now that Adam was listening to his body more, he received the message clearly. Battle was coming.

"You love this Earthling?" Todd asked.

Adam hated to admit it when his senses were warning him of danger, but he had to. "Yes."

"Then I'd like to meet her."

"I don't see why that would be necessary."

"It is necessary," Todd said. "I have to decide if this is some sort of ruse to allow you to stay. The High Council won't just take your word that you fell in love with an Earthling during your leave."

They should. Adam's teeth started to hurt from grinding together. Adam had done so much for the Coalition, he'd worked directly with the High Council for years. If they didn't trust him, they didn't trust anyone.

The thought didn't sit well with him on many levels. If they didn't understand trust, he might be better served to put his faith elsewhere, like in himself. And in Evelyn.

"I'll arrange a meeting," Adam said.

The first volley had been fired, but Todd didn't understand who he was dealing with. Adam would set up the meeting in a safe location that he scouted in advance. But before he brought Evelyn anywhere near Todd, Adam needed to arm himself with information.

A weapon would have been preferable, but if he was caught planet-side with one, the High Council would certainly refuse his request to stay. Adam needed to call his crew and get them working on this. He needed to know exactly how deep of water Todd was treading.

Chapter Seven

Getting engaged was not good for concentration. Neither was incredible sex. Evelyn stared blankly at the pages of the journals she was supposed to be indexing for about an hour. Her body tingled from the memory of Adam's touch as her mind replayed vivid scenes from their morning together.

Nope, she wasn't getting anything done today.

Maybe a walk in the park would be nice. She decided to go back to where it had all begun, to the very bench where she and Adam shared their first kiss.

The day wasn't getting any cooler, but the bench was still shaded from the afternoon sun. She sat and closed her eyes, smiling as she thought about their morning.

"I don't suppose you'd like some company?"

Evelyn jumped at the unexpected voice—the unexpectedly close voice.

A tall man stood before her. He was wearing a charcoal gray suit that fit his lithe frame perfectly, accenting his narrow waist and broad shoulders. His nose was straight and thin, like his lips, and his cheekbones were high and sharp. His dark hair was combed back from his face and full of enough product to be formed into a perfect helmet.

If it wasn't for the aura of douchery he was giving off, he might have been handsome in an avant-garde supermodel sort of way. As it was, Evelyn could only think one thing as she looked at him.

"How are you not dying?" she said.

He blinked, a momentary lowering of his eyebrows and curling of his lip making her more than a little uncomfortable. He covered the expression quickly with a smile as fake as a mannequin's. That plus the hair-helmet and she actually let out a little laugh.

He didn't look like a real person. It was more like he'd been stamped out from a plastic mold.

"I'm afraid I don't follow you," he said.

"You're in a dark three-piece suit in hundred degree weather and you're not even sweating. That's weird." She shook her head and said, "I don't mean to be rude. I'm just having a really awesome day and my verbal filters are even lower than usual."

This time, he let his sneer stay a bit longer. When he pasted a smile on his face again, he accompanied it with lowered eyelids. He sat next to her, sliding his arm behind her on the bench.

"A good mood is nothing to apologize for," he said. "And good days should be celebrated."

Evelyn scooted forward on the bench and turned to face

him more fully, trying to figure out what the hell was going on. Heavy eyes, half-smirk on the mouth, lips a little pouty, body angled forward…

"Oh my God. You're hitting on me," she said.

The extremely strange stranger sat back quickly, scowling again. This guy was not good at hiding his emotions. His smile was a little more genuine when it returned, but there was a reptilian vibe to it that made the hair on the back of her neck prick up in warning.

"Maybe I am," he said. "Would that be such a bad thing?"

"I guess it's true what they say about getting more attention after you're engaged. Which, I am. As of today. Hence, the super-awesome day."

"Even more reason to celebrate." He leaned forward a bit, and Evelyn scooted back further.

She held up her hands and said, "Ho there, cowboy. Ease up on the spurs."

Now he looked genuinely confused. "What?"

"I'm not sure where that came from. But I do know where I'm going. Which is away. From you. Right now. You have crazy-eyes. Seriously—you're creeping me out."

She managed to get a few steps from the bench before Mr. Mannequin called out to her.

"Is that really such a good idea, Evelyn? Making a good impression on Adam's liaison will go a long way toward helping his paperwork through."

Thoughts raced through her head. Liaison? Was this the lanky guy Adam had been arguing with earlier?

She turned back around to gape at the man. Tall, thin, dark hair. Yeah, he could be the same guy. Same expensive suit, anyway.

"Wait," she said. "You're not telling me I have to have sex with you for you to put Adam's paperwork through, right? Because if you are, I will find whatever authorities I need to report you to and—"

"Please." The liaison stood up, contempt practically rolling off him. Shaking out his jacket, he smoothed his hands down his lapel and then straightened his tie. "I have my pick of women. Why would I want you?"

Evelyn felt his words ping off her ego like pebbles thrown by a wayward child. The little girl with braces and acne she had once been was now dating the quarterback of the football team—and the head of science club—all in one delicious package.

"Is this some kind of test to see if I'm actually in love with Adam?" she asked. "Because it's a pretty shitty test. I'm just saying."

"Your feelings are insignificant. Just like the wayward glitch whose been leading you on."

Despite herself, a small ember of doubt lit in her mind. Adam wasn't leading her on. He loved her. She was sure of that.

"First of all, Adam is not a glitch. He is awesome.

Second, I'm pretty sure I can find a lawyer who will be happy to turn this festival of bad manners into a case for letting Adam stay here no matter what a petty bureaucrat with delusions of grandeur has to say."

"You really have no idea who you've been fucking, do you?"

"Language! There are kids in this park sometimes." Evelyn was growing increasingly uncomfortable with this guy.

It was broad daylight, and they were near the entrance to the park. She could see a few people on the other side of the pond. They were out of earshot for a regular conversation, but if she started to scream, she wouldn't be in this alone.

"What does he see in you?" the liaison said. "I suppose it's impossible to understand the reasoning of a madman."

"I certainly am not following." She made little gestures with her hands as she explained her joke. "See what I did there? I'm actually implying that *you're* the madman."

The liaison slid his chin to the side, as if he was chewing on something. Evelyn had the weirdest idea that he was going to unhinge his jaw and swallow her whole. She took a step back, and he smiled.

"That's right, little monkey. Be afraid of me. But the person you should really be afraid of is Adam."

He slid his hands into his pockets, suddenly smug— which made her even more nervous. He could have anything in there. Mace. Bear mace. A teeny tiny gun. She should probably be more cautious, but he was seriously pushing her buttons.

"You're not making any sense," she said.

"Let me use smaller words for your primitive mind. Adam is lying to you."

Evelyn didn't buy it. She crossed her arms and jutted her chin at the liaison. "About what?"

"Who he is. Where he's from."

"Aha! He hasn't told me where he's from, so how is that a lie?"

"And you say you're going to marry him? Do you even know his full name?"

"Adam Smith." She'd have to ask Adam his middle name the next time she saw him.

A tiny sliver of misgiving crossed her mind. Saying Adam's name aloud… It sounded kind of fake.

"'Adam Smith' is a cover identity I made for him when he decided he had to see this backwater during his shore leave. Didn't know that, either, did you? Your love is military. A General responsible for the deaths of billions."

"Okay, wackadoodle. Now I know you're crazy. I think that would have made the news, given that there are only seven billion people on the entire planet."

"On *this* planet."

"Just so you know, this is the part of the conversation where I run away screaming for help."

The liaison pulled a small silver disk from his pocket and squeezed it with his thumb. Evelyn told her body to turn and run, but she couldn't move. She felt suspended, as if not even gravity was pulling her down. Some other force —something she didn't have a name for—was holding her in place. Her stomach lurched at the bizarre weightlessness that her brain couldn't manage to process.

"Now you're going to be quiet and listen to me, *monkey*," the man said. "And then you can tell me if you think your precious glitch is worth all this trouble."

Chapter Eight

"Open a secure channel with K-35-b7." Adam paced within the small space of his skimmer, an uncomfortable energy coursing through him that he was unfamiliar with. His skin was crawling with the need for action.

This was a new battlefield for him.

The viewscreen that took up most of the main wall of the craft flickered to life, his second-in-command filling it. Around the edges of Khel's blond hair, Adam could see weapons hanging on the wall. A familiar plasma rifle and a wickedly curved blade.

My command room.

"General Serath," Khel said.

Adam felt a chill at hearing his true name after so long. He pushed through the discomfort.

"Khel." Adam nodded toward the screen.

Khel was a glitch, like Adam, but even taller and thick with muscle. Adam had reviewed Khel's file thoroughly, and still shuddered at the thought of all the tests they had put the man through to understand what had gone wrong with his genetic engineering.

"Activate a full link with the *Arbiter's* computer and that of my skimmer using maximum security protocols," Adam commanded.

"Yes, sir." Khel's arms moved outside of the area Adam could see. After a few moments, Khel leaned back and said, "It's done."

Adam crossed to the viewscreen and began entering commands at the control panel at its side. A smaller, transparent screen appeared within his communications window with Khel, providing data on the *Arbiter's* status and location.

"You're three days out from the Sol system," Adam said.

They would arrive exactly when Adam's shore leave ended. Khel was nothing if not efficient.

"At standard speed." Khel's blue eyes glimmered with something akin to hope. "Do you need us to expedite your retrieval?"

"Tired of command already?"

Khel didn't pick up on Adam's joke. It wasn't surprising, since Adam had never made one before visiting Earth.

"The *Arbiter* is not as effective without you at command," Khel said. "The crew is eager for your return."

The crew had no idea Adam was thinking about leaving the fleet. Khel…would not take that well. Adam needed to keep his focus on the matter at hand.

"That must wait," Adam said. "I need a full report on

Earth's planetary liaison."

Khel's mouth opened and closed a few times. "Sir?"

"Something is very, very wrong here," Adam said. "And Todd Simms is at the center of it."

"T-14-b5." Khel again shifted as his hands slid over the controls back on the *Arbiter*, feeding data to Adam's skimmer through the secure link.

Adam almost wished he was back on board. Though he could investigate the matter remotely, it would be much easier to mete out punishment if he had the resources of the *Arbiter* at hand—and he was certain there would be a severe penalty for what Todd was doing.

An abrasive buzz brought Adam's attention back to the viewscreen. Khel's pale eyebrows were furrowed.

"Report," Adam said.

Khel shook his head. "This makes no sense. His file is locked. My security codes can't grant me access."

"That's not possible." Adam stopped reviewing the scrolling data Khel was feeding him and entered his own security code.

Nothing happened.

Adam's heart felt as though it had turned to lead. He was the highest ranking military officer in the fleet. The only people in the entire Coalition of Planets who could restrict his access to information on other citizens was the High Council itself. But they wouldn't concern themselves with such a small planet...

Something else had to be going on. Todd must have connections that Adam didn't suspect. Which meant he was even more dangerous than Adam feared.

Evelyn…

"General?" Khel prompted.

"The soldier assigned to Earth's listening station has been sending regular reports, correct?" Adam said.

Khel tapped on his control panel a few times. The furrow between his eyebrows deepened.

"Records indicate there is no soldier assigned to Earth's listening station," he said. "All reports have come directly from the planetary liaison."

"That's against protocol," Adam nearly shouted.

He couldn't believe what he was hearing. No matter who Todd Simms was connected to, the High Council would not stand for this.

"We'll have to gather data through other channels," Adam said. "Put Ari and Vay on this. With his investigative expertise and her cultural knowledge, they should be able to find something useful. Just be sure they know to proceed with the utmost discretion. They are to report to you and I and no other, understood?"

Khel nodded briskly. "Understood. Should we increase our speed?"

"Yes. I want to see how deep his connections are," Adam said. "Let's see if he learns of your expedited schedule. I'll be in contact with you soon."

Adam tapped the command to end the transmission, his dread growing.

He had to check on Evelyn. After confronting Todd earlier, Adam didn't know what the man was capable of. He ran from the ship, only pausing for long enough to make sure that the cloaking field was in place before tearing through the forest toward Evelyn's apartment building.

She didn't live far from the park. Adam reached her dwelling in less than half an hour, sweating and out of breath. He unlocked Evelyn's apartment with the key she'd given him.

Her purse was on the side table just inside her apartment. Adam locked the door behind him, then set his key and wallet next to her belongings. He took a moment to look at them jumbled together. This simple domesticity was supposed to be his future, and now, he was fearful for her life.

Normally, she would be sitting at the computer desk in the area adjacent to her kitchen, but she wasn't there or on the couch. The kitchen was quiet—which left the bedroom.

He walked briskly down the hallway, eager to see her again.

"Evelyn, I…"

He paused in the doorway to her room. Evelyn was sitting at the foot of her bed, hands clasped in her lap. Her glasses were low on her nose and she hadn't bothered to push them back into place. She was staring blankly at the floor in front of her.

Adam's throat seemed to close. Something was very wrong. He practically leapt into the room, then knelt at her feet.

"Evelyn, what's happened?"

Her eyes were glazed when she turned to him, not the bright, sharp gaze he was used to. She almost looked as if she'd had a mind-wipe.

Cygnus X, it couldn't be.

"I met your liaison today," she said.

Rage surged through him. What had Todd done to her? And how could Adam not have thought to protect her sooner?

"What did he do?" Adam asked.

She must have read the guilt on his face. Her eyes focused and the brightness seeped back into them, fueled by anger. Adam felt hope flutter in his chest. He knew this Evelyn. And—thank the stars—she knew him.

"It's my turn to ask the questions. Here's the first one." Her brows drew down on her forehead, her lips pulled into a frown, and she pushed her glasses up the bridge of her nose forcefully. "Are you an alien?"

Adam felt as if the ground had given way beneath him and he was free-falling. Not since his first zero-g maneuvers had he been this disoriented.

His stomach was ricocheting against his ribs, his heart frantically looking for escape. His mind whirled pointlessly, offering nothing helpful, except the one word that escaped his lips.

"Yes."

She shoved him, hard. He was surprised by her strength and already off-balance enough that he toppled over. She leapt up, towering over him, hands clenched into fists at her sides. For a moment, he wondered if she was going to kick him where he lay.

"You jerk," she yelled. "I can't believe I actually fell for your scheme. You used me!"

"What are you talking about?"

"You want to stay on Earth so bad you'll do anything, even marry me." Her voice hitched on the words, but rage quickly pushed aside any sorrow on her features.

"You've got it backwards."

"Right, because I'm just a stupid, un-evolved, hairless monkey from a backwater planet that's as rich in resources as it is lacking in technology."

The sentiment was all too familiar. Damn him, Todd must have told her so much. Things that were forbidden for an Earthling to know.

This was Todd's plan. He was setting them up, trying to make the High Council mandate a mind-wipe. They might even decide to take *all* of her memories of Adam.

But he and Evelyn could fight this, as long as they fought together. Adam needed her by his side.

"That's not true." He tried to get through to her with the

humor she had taught him. "Besides, don't Earthlings think they evolved from primates rather than monkeys?"

"I swear, I will kick you in your teeth."

Her voice was deadly calm, but she was talking to him, at least. He could get through to her. He had to.

She started pacing back and forth, pulling strands of hair loose from her ponytail. "Earthlings! God, I'm just an Earthling to you!"

"You're not *just* anything to me. You're the woman I plan to marry. The woman I love."

"Drop it! I know you're just trying to get your Gray card."

"Gray card?"

She stopped pacing and lifted one shoulder in a half-shrug, a crack in her defenses opening that Adam desperately needed to navigate. Her voice lost a bit of its edge. She was falling back on humor, as always.

"Like a green card, but for aliens."

He remembered the tiny gray creatures in so many of the TV shows and movies she had shown him. Grays.

Adam couldn't help himself—he started to laugh. He laughed so hard that tears streamed down his face.

"It wasn't that funny," she said.

Pulling himself together, he managed to stand, wiping at his eyes. "How can you say something like that and still doubt why I want to marry you?"

She lifted her chin, eyes blazing. "What, that I'm not

funny?"

Adam took a deep breath, then let it out slowly. He was going to set this right.

"You are hilarious," he said. "You are ridiculous. Absurd."

"Such flattery. How could I possibly resist you?"

He dared to reach out and gently cup her elbows. She didn't pull away, but she did look like she might head-butt him. She had even more fire than he knew.

"You are completely unpredictable," he said. "You make me look at the universe with new eyes. You make me laugh at myself, at everything. You taught me how to enjoy life rather than just existing. You think I want to marry you to stay on Earth? I don't give a damn where we are. I just want to be with you."

Her lips softened ever so slightly. He might not have noticed at all, except he was having trouble not staring at them. She let out a sigh and her arms relaxed a bit in his grip.

"Were you ever going to tell me? Maybe after the first kid came out green?"

"Wouldn't she be gray?"

That earned him the faintest glimmer of a smile.

The time for dissembling was over. If Todd had stepped on the mine of telling Evelyn they were aliens, there wasn't any more damage Adam could do. And there was plenty he could fix.

She pushed her glasses up her nose and crossed her arms again. He was expecting more questions about his origins, so was surprised when Evelyn said, "She?"

What a thing for her to focus on. It made his heart pound, his stomach fill with butterflies. His life with her would be full of laughter and wonder, love and family. He was certain of it.

"Or he. As long as it's a surprise, I don't care."

"It usually is with us monkeys. You'll just be lucky if you get out of the delivery room without me throwing poop at you."

"Gross. And again—inaccurate. You aren't a monkey, or did Todd neglect to mention your origins?"

"He had plenty to say on other topics."

Adam didn't doubt it. "Humans did evolve from something resembling a primate, but not on this planet."

Her eyes widened and her lips parted. That caught her attention. "Where did we evolve, then?"

"Sadr-4. We're from the same planet. Millennia ago, a colony ship went off course and crashed here."

"That's not in any of our history books."

"Their ship was destroyed and they had no means of manufacturing anything. Survival, dealing with an alien world, vying for resources with the already-evolving Earth hominids—that closely resembled our own ancestors... I think they had plenty to handle. Their origins just got lost along the way."

"Hence lost colony?"

"Exactly."

"So you and I are the same species?"

"Fundamentally. Our DNA has just been a bit...altered."

"Altered how?" She stared at his chest and leaned a little closer, unclasping her arms so she could gently tug on his shirt. "I didn't notice anything out of place earlier."

"You wouldn't. Everything is in order and carefully controlled. Geneticists take care of all the details of childbirth in the Coalition of Planets."

"*All* the details?"

"Yes. Women don't want to deal with the pain and discomfort of carrying children in their bodies when they and their partner can just place an order for exactly what they want." In most cases.

"Your parents must have been thrilled with you," she said.

"Actually..." He swallowed hard, struggling to speak the words. But she needed to know. "I'm considered defective. The command abilities my parents requested came through, so I'm of great use in the military, but physically... I don't exactly fit in at most Coalition social events. That's one of the reasons I prefer life on a ship. My parents received a full refund."

Her eyes snapped to his, anger sparking in their loamy depths. Adam hadn't previously felt the pain of his parents' rejection the way he did in that moment—one of the downsides of becoming more aware of his feelings. Looking into Evelyn's soulful eyes—connecting with the empathy he saw there—made it worth it.

"That's awful," she said.

"It's just the way things are. My society isn't as emotional as yours. Or as physical."

"Not as physical, huh?" She smiled briefly. The distance he felt between them was narrowing, but he hadn't quite closed the gap yet.

"As you discovered. We still have sexual urges, but there are many other things vying for attention. And the biological drive to reproduce has been rendered obsolete. The Coalition has developed various chemical solutions that meet most of the emotional and physical needs of our citizens."

"You mean people take drugs instead of having sex?"

"Quite often. But if the drugs don't satisfy the person's drives, they find like-minded individuals and have sex with the assistance of *Coupling*."

"Coupling?"

"The chemical mix that facilitates sex. It takes the body through the entire process within a few minutes, from arousal through orgasm." Adam couldn't believe how easy it was to talk to her about this. He hadn't even spoken so frankly with the women he'd used *Coupling* with. "People most often use it alone, but if taken with a partner, the drug does all the work for us. We have to act quickly to keep pace with it, in fact."

"How romantic," she said. "And you've only ever had sex while taking it?"

"It would be unheard of to attempt sex without it. I was already seen as unusual for preferring sex with a partner. I suppose I'm something of a throwback in more ways than one."

She slid her arms around his neck and leaned forward until their chests were touching. "You have to love the classics."

"Do you?" Adam had clearly stated his feelings and intentions, but she had yet to say those words back to him. He knew he wouldn't truly rest until he heard them. Until he knew for sure.

"Love you?" Her face relaxed and the warmth flowed back into her smile. He felt as if his heart had stopped.

"I do," she said. "I love you, Adam Smith. Whatever your name really is."

Chapter Nine

If Evelyn doubted Adam's feelings before, all of that was wiped away by the expression on his face when she told him she loved him. His eyes softened, his lips parted, and he looked at her as if he couldn't believe what she was saying.

They really had it bad for each other.

He lifted his hands to her face, tracing his thumbs over her cheekbones, then leaned forward and gently pressed his lips to hers. It wasn't long before his mouth became more insistent. His hand slid around her waist, pulling her closer.

Evelyn tightened her grip on Adam's neck, reveling in every feeling. She didn't wait for an invitation, but trailed her tongue along his lips until he opened his mouth to her. His tongue met hers, thrust for hungry thrust.

He gripped her ass, rocking her against his erection. He parted from her for a moment—just long enough to lift her shirt and pull it over her head, then fling it away. Thankfully, she had put on her best bra before going to the University. He ran his fingertips over the lacy fabric.

"How do I get this off of you?"

"There's a clasp in the back."

"Turn around."

"Is that an order, General?" She had meant it as a playful tease, but a shadow crossed his expression.

"What else did Todd tell you about me?"

"Nothing that we need to discuss right now." She brought her hands to Adam's face, running the backs of her fingers along his cheek. "I know you're a good man, whatever planet you're from or rank you hold."

"I'm not proud of everything that I've done, but most of my missions were about keeping the peace. It's important to me that you know that. And most of those missions, the people that I stopped..."

She moved her hands to the back of his head. "We have time. I want to know everything about you. But right now, I need this."

She dragged his lips back to hers, kissing him deeply. Grabbing his shoulders, she turned him around so he was standing at the foot of her bed, then gave him a shove. He went along with it, sitting down on the bed hard and falling back on his elbows.

"Now, can we please stop talking?" she asked. "I have much more interesting things in mind for us to do."

She reached behind her back and unfastened the clasp of her bra, then smirked as she pulled the lacy garment off and threw it aside. His gaze locked on her breasts and he nodded.

"Very good," she said. "I hope you're as good at taking orders as giving them."

Adam grinned, then leaned forward and wrapped his arms around her waist. "I'm yours to command."

"Oh, I really like the sound of that."

She ran her fingers through his dark hair. It was so soft. That was probably part of his DNA. She tried not to think too much about that—all the implications associated with his origins.

Evelyn wasn't close with her parents, mostly because they didn't understand a word she said. But they loved each other. The idea of being grown in a petri dish, and then returned to sender…was just too terrible.

"I can't say that I like your expression right now," Adam said.

"I'm not obeying my own orders. Now is not the time for thinking."

"What is it the time for?" He gave her a gentle smile, his hands slowly roving over her back.

"Kissing would be good."

"Where shall I kiss you?" He started to work the front of her jeans, undoing the button and slowly pulling down the zipper.

"Like I said, you have really good instincts."

"In that case, there's something I've wanted to do."

He leaned forward and clasped one nipple in his mouth, flicking his tongue over the surface until it tightened.

Evelyn gasped, burying her hands more deeply in his hair and hugging his head to her chest. She kicked off her shoes as he slowly worked her jeans down over her hips, taking her panties with them.

He moved to her other breast, teasing, kneading, caressing. Her body ached for more. She wanted him all over her, inside her.

As if he sensed her need, he slid his hand between her legs, two fingers gliding effortlessly into her while his thumb traced lazy circles around her clitoris. She grabbed his shoulders to keep her balance.

"I'm going to fall over if you keep doing that."

"I'll catch you."

Her smile transformed to a gasp as he hit a particularly sensitive spot. "Oh God, that feels so good."

"Then let me keep doing it."

Warmth coursed through her body where his hands were working. At some point, she wasn't even sure when, he put his other arm behind her, helping to hold her up.

"I want more," she said. "All of you. Now."

Her body ached as he pulled his hands from her and stood. He unfastened his pants and pulled out his dick, barely pausing as he picked her up and spun them around.

Her knees hit the edge of her bed and she let herself fall back. Adam followed, covering her body with his. He reached between them to guide himself to her core, then buried himself to the hilt with a groan of pleasure.

Or maybe it was hers. It was hard to tell, and she didn't really care to sort it out.

He immediately started thrusting deep. No preludes, no hesitation. Evelyn wanted to give him more. New sensations, new pleasures.

She wrapped her thighs around his waist so he had even better access, and raked her fingernails down his back. She felt his shiver with every part of her, everywhere they touched.

The valley of his spine seemed particularly sensitive. She trailed her fingers down the length of it, splaying her hands over his ass and squeezing the muscles that were rhythmically contracting—pushing him deep within her, pulling out to the protest of her body.

Her body was lighting up everywhere. She must be glowing. No one could feel this good—this energized, this ready to explode—without glowing.

"Moons, Evelyn," he grunted out. "That feels...too good."

He kissed her before she could respond, so she dug her nails into him, playing with the threshold between pleasure and pain. He rewarded her by pushing himself up on his hands and angling his hips to grind against her clitoris with every thrust.

The fireworks began, small explosions at first, that quickly built into a cascade of color and energy, making every cell in her body feel alive.

"Adam!"

His own cry mingled with hers as his thrusts became more desperate, uncontrolled, the force of them rocking the bed. Her body clenched tightly around him, joining the pulsing of his shaft.

He buried himself deep and stayed there, head back, eyes tightly shut, a look of such rapture on his face she knew she'd never be able to forget it. The thudding of her heart in her ears slowly subsided, tension she hadn't noticed melting away into the mattress beneath her.

Adam lowered himself to his elbows, careful not to put too much of his weight on her as he had the first time. He nuzzled her ear, nibbling on her earlobe and kissing her neck.

"We need to keep doing that forever." It took several breaths to get out her sentence, but she managed it.

"Absolutely."

He rocked against her again, kissing her deeply. She could feel him softening inside of her, her body no longer stretching as much to hold onto him. He didn't seem willing to end their union, which was fine with her. The relaxed connection was wonderful in its own way.

They were going to get married. The thought sprang up unexpected, but no longer accompanied by surprise.

This felt right. The two of them together. It was how the universe was meant to be. She was sure of it—could feel it in her bones.

They just had to convince the insane liaison to let Adam stay.

Chapter Ten

"I want to see your ship."

When Evelyn made the request, Adam was hardly in a state to refuse her anything. A shiver flowed over his skin as he thought of the warmth of her body. There was nothing like the incredible feeling of belonging and connection when he was inside of her, their arms around each other, holding each other as close as they possibly could.

He felt like he was melting into her sometimes, a union beyond anything he'd experienced. Remembering that and enjoying the forest around him, he could almost forget about the challenges they faced.

In the full bloom of summer, the trees overhead were thick with rich green foliage. Insects that couldn't bite off his head chirred pleasantly around them and birds called out to each other. The entirely wholesome sound of dirt and rocks crunching beneath their boots blended in with the woodland melody. The only thing that would have improved the hike was if they could hold hands, but the trail was too narrow for that.

"Earth to Adam." She laughed. "I guess I should say,

'Sadr-4 to Adam.'"

"I have no idea what you're talking about." He smiled anyway, delighting in learning a new game. She was the most playful being he had ever encountered.

"It's an expression we Earth-humans use for when the person we're with seems to be zoning out. I guess that idiom was overlooked when you learned English."

"A few were. I am a bit distracted. Bringing you to my ship is a big deal."

"Why do it, then?"

"Because you asked."

That and because he needed to check on Khel's progress investigating Todd Simms. Adam's ship held all of his weapons as well. He would feel safer once Evelyn was on board. Perhaps she should even remain there with him until everything was sorted out.

"So..." Evelyn said. "If I asked you to throw me down on the ground and have sex with me right here and now, you'd do that too?"

Adam stopped so suddenly that she ran into his back. Making love to her in the forest? Could they really do that? His body grew hard at the thought of Evelyn in a green field, the wind playing over their naked bodies as...

"Do not get your hopes up!" she said. "I shouldn't have used that as an example." She slipped past him, hands held up as if to fend him off, but she was smiling. "It is amazing enough that you've been getting me out in the wilderness so much that this hike isn't making me wheeze. I am not ready to throw down with you in a field full of bugs and dirt."

"Not ready *yet*." Adam grinned at her as she gave him a fake look of disapproval over her shoulder.

His body slowly got the message that now was the time to walk, as disappointing as that was. She wasn't too far ahead as he resumed his trek toward the ship.

"It is awesome to know the actual location of another inhabited planet," she said. "And so close."

"The Milky Way is much more populated than you think. There are protocols in place to keep Earth from figuring that out."

"What kind of protocols?"

"There are teams assigned to all the planets with preservation status. They do what's necessary to allow any sentient inhabitants—even ones that originated from a lost colony—to develop along their own natural progression without gaining too much knowledge too quickly. Earth also has a listening station in orbit. Cloaked from detection, of course."

He was concerned that there wasn't a Coalition soldier assigned to Earth's listening station yet. It was most likely an intentional oversight by the planetary liaison—to protect his operations on Earth. Adam would be certain that his crew downloaded the memory banks of the listening station before departing, though he was certain Todd had altered the data to reflect what he wished for it to say.

"Wait, so you guys are stopping us from realizing that aliens are real?" Evelyn said.

"We're stopping you from getting hard evidence. Can you imagine the panic that would ensue if everyone suddenly discovered that not only were they not alone in the universe, but they're right next to a galactic highway?"

She stopped to stare at him, wide-eyed. "Are we?"

"It's close."

"I'm glad you guys decided to go around the planet instead of through it when you set that up."

She grinned in the particular way that let him know she was referencing a sci-fi story that he hadn't experienced yet. They had a lifetime for her to share everything with him. He couldn't wait to get started.

Evelyn turned around and resumed picking her way along the barely discernible trail that led to his skimmer. When she started to get off course, he corrected her with a gentle touch.

"It's still pretty shitty of you guys to decide that for us," she said. "Somebody should give the powers that be a talking-to. Maybe you could do that when this is all settled."

Adam was glad she wasn't looking at him in that moment. He didn't say anything, not wanting to lie and not wanting to let her know the truth. If the High Council let him relinquish his citizenship—to become an Earthling himself—he would never be allowed to leave the planet again.

He didn't care. Space was cold and uninviting. Evelyn was everything he had wanted his entire life. Warmth, connection, love.

And her homeworld was so full of life, just like her. He would gladly live out his time on Earth, perhaps have some children with her—naturally, having no idea what they would be like.

The thought made his breath catch in his chest. Children. Natural children—not designed in a lab or ordered from a catalog. Moons, he wanted that. Desperately. Immediately.

"You're falling behind." She turned to look at him, a slight crease between her eyebrows. "Are you okay?"

"Children. I want children."

She smiled and put her hands on her hips. "What, like now? Because I told you, I'm not having sex in a forest. We can talk about me going off birth control after we're married. We have other concerns at the moment."

"You do want them though, right?"

"Eventually, sure. I'd love a few rugrats underfoot. But you need to keep your head in the game until we've dealt with the liaison."

She turned back to the trail, taking a few steps before he caught her up by her waist and lifted her into the air. Her laughter rang through the trees, startling some nearby birds.

"No sex in the forest!" she yelled.

"I know." He set her on her feet. He wanted to kiss her, but if he did, he wasn't sure he'd be able to stop. "What about sex on my ship?"

Evelyn glanced over her shoulder at him, eyes widening and lips parting as if she was about to speak. Instead, she pushed his arms away from her waist and bolted up the trail. Adam followed, laughing all the way.

Chapter Eleven

In the center of a clearing filled with green grass, the most beautiful vehicle that Evelyn had ever seen perched like a resting bird of prey. The exterior was black, polished to a high sheen. Two wings stretched from the ship's underbelly, curving down toward the earth in graceful arcs. Four legs held it up from the ground.

Adam said it was a skimmer, but it didn't have a name past that. She wanted to name it right then, but could only come up with ridiculous things like, *Starshadow*.

She waited at the edge of the clearing as Adam approached the vessel. His gait changed as he grew nearer to it, shoulders more squared, spine stiff, hands curling into fists. His demeanor put off an energy of command that she found both incredibly sexy and a little intimidating.

He lifted a hand to his ship, and as soon as he touched it a line appeared in the smooth skin of the hull. The line was joined by two others forming part of a rectangle. When it started lowering, she realized it was a ramp.

Adam gestured to the opening. "Well? You wanted to see my ship."

"Right."

He reached out to her, his smile softening. "Come on."

She smiled back, then ran across the clearing. She was about to go on board an actual spaceship. An *alien* spaceship. She'd dreamt of this moment her whole life.

Still, she wasn't sure which was causing her heart to thump in her chest—the ship, or the man whose warm hand clasped hers.

"Is this why we never hiked in this section of the park?" she asked.

"If I came too close, the cloak would turn off automatically. Besides, there were plenty of other places to explore."

"I'm only interested in exploring this at the moment."

"By all means." He led her up the ramp and onto the ship.

The interior was small. He had told her it was a one-person ship and pared down to the barest essentials. The Coalition didn't want their technology accidentally falling into the wrong hands, after all. Skimmers had just enough to get people to their destination and back.

The walls were white, the floor was gray, and everything was made of metal. Evelyn had a momentary bout of claustrophobia. Adam's love of the outdoors made more sense after seeing his ship. If he spent all of his time in places like this, an open horizon would be a welcome change.

The walls had what looked at first like designs engraved on them, but eventually she realized they were controls. Indentations that might be hand-holds seemed to accompany a few stations she could make out.

"There are no chairs," she said.

"We need to stay alert while we're on duty, so there aren't any."

"Are we just going to do it on the floor, then?"

His grin was huge. Her body began to tingle thinking of other huge parts of him.

"There's a sleeping chamber up that ladder," he said.

She turned to look where he was pointing and sure enough there were hand and footholds recessed into the wall leading up to a hatch in the ceiling.

"How do you work the controls if you need to use your hands to hold on?"

"We have artificial gravity. For safety, we also hook up to harnesses during shifts to keep us in place in the event of power loss."

"That is so cool."

Evelyn didn't dare ask to take the ship for a spin. She wasn't even sure if Adam was supposed to fly it during his vacation when he was by himself, let alone showing off technology for Earthlings. She asked one of her many other questions instead.

"Are you going to get in trouble for bringing me here?" It was at the top of her mind.

"The liaison is the one on the disintegration pad. I still can't believe that he told you about us. That is a serious crime."

"Are you going to report him?"

One of Adam's shoulders lifted slightly. "I'm looking into it."

"What aren't you telling me? I know when you're keeping me in the dark."

"The liaison—Todd—is dangerous. Telling you about us and showing you some of our technology might be the least of his crimes. I have my crew looking into it, but until the situation is resolved, I don't want you to be alone."

"If Todd wants to get to me, I doubt a crowd will stop him."

"I was thinking I'd stay with you."

She finished her circuit of the ship, then walked to Adam and wrapped her arms around his neck. "My own personal bodyguard. I like the sound of that."

"Guarding your body is only one of the things I have planned."

He slid his hands around her waist and pulled her close, pressing his lips to hers. He smelled so good—like fresh cut grass and peppermint. His hands roved to her ass, lifting her slightly and pressing her against him.

She pushed away from him, then started backing toward the ladder that led to the sleeping chamber. "Why don't you show me the rest of your ship?"

He didn't answer and didn't follow her. In fact, he didn't move at all.

"Adam?"

He was standing completely still, his face a mask of fear. When she reached out to him, a sharp pain tore through her fingers. She shook her hand, tingling jolts of energy shooting up her arm.

"I wouldn't try that again. Unless you're okay with losing the use of that hand."

Her heart sank at the voice behind her. Todd.

When she turned, she wasn't surprised to see him holding the same shiny disk that he'd used on her in the park. His other hand held an ordinary gun.

"I just don't see the allure." Todd shook his head, his gaze traveling over her body. "Unless you have certain skills that add to your worth. After I deal with the General, maybe I'll do a few experiments of my own."

Evelyn glanced at Adam, took in the anguish and rage on his features, and knew she was on her own. She looked around the ship, but there were no weapons lying around. The only escape was the open ramp, which led to the expanse of forest beyond. Help was miles away.

"Yes, monkey. You are trapped. Let the panic seep in." Todd kept his gun pointed at her, but turned to address Adam. "Did you really think I would believe you were giving up everything for *her*? You arrogant glitch. I wish I could let you live to regret sticking your nose into my operations."

"You can't kill him!" Evelyn stepped forward, but stopped when Todd raised his weapon higher, sighting her down the barrel. She held up her hands and said, "How will you explain his death to your superiors?"

"When I deliver his corpse to the High Council, they're going to give me a medal for protecting Earth from his conquest."

"You're delusional." She was baiting him on purpose, keeping him talking, gathering information, trying to find anything that might help get her and Adam out of this.

"You're the only one who's delusional here. You really think that he's doing this for you?" Todd's lip curled in a sneer and he tilted his head away, as if he could barely stand to look at her. At least he lowered his gun a bit. "A General decides to suddenly leave his prosperous career, give up his citizenship, and relinquish the vast resources he's accumulated over decades of successful campaigns to live on a primitive world where he'll have no access to real technology and can never leave the planet again? He's not after you. He wants Earth. But I got here first."

"You can't leave?" Evelyn turned to Adam, not believing Todd's words. "If you stayed with me, you were going to give all that up?"

Adam's brow furrowed slightly and his eyes narrowed.

It was true. And he wasn't going to tell her. He was planning to give up everything to be with her and he wasn't even going to let her know what he was sacrificing.

"With the riches this planet possesses, it would be more than a fair trade," Todd said.

Evelyn closed her eyes, visualizing the situation, trying to find a way out. On board, there was nothing to help her. But outside the ship there were plenty of thick, heavy branches perfect for thumping an insane alien over the head with. She only had to manage to get outside and sneak back in without Todd realizing it.

Right. Only that.

The first step was getting out without getting killed. Playing along with Todd's story seemed her best bet. She only hoped that Adam would realize she was acting.

"I can't believe you would do this to me!" Evelyn bit her fist for effect. She doubted Todd had watched any 50s sci-fi movies where the women were constantly doing ridiculous things like that. "After everything we did... And it was all a lie!"

"Stop yelling!" Todd lifted his gun again, pointing it right at her face.

"I'm sorry, I just... I'm so emotional right now." As she'd hoped, Todd's sneer deepened. He looked a little green. "I don't want anything to do with this! Do whatever you want to him. I just want to go home. I promise, I won't tell anyone that aliens are real."

Todd stared at her for a moment, then his thin lips pulled into a smile. "No, you should tell them. Waste your life trying to convince people that aliens are real. That will be so much more amusing than just killing you. Go on."

He shooed her with his gun. Evelyn wasn't sure if he was baiting her, trying to get her to turn around so he could shoot her in the back—but it was the best chance she had. She turned and bolted, heart pounding in her chest.

She could hardly believe it when she reached the trees. Pausing, she looked back at the ship, but didn't see Todd watching her. Adrenaline flooded her system, making her lightheaded.

She didn't have time for that. Focusing with all her will, she started looking for a branch that she could use as a weapon. It didn't take long to find one solid enough to do damage, but small enough to wield.

She wanted to run back to the ship as fast as she could, but surprise was crucial. She only prayed that Todd would do more grandstanding before killing Adam.

Tears burned her eyes, but she blinked them away. Adam needed her. There was still hope.

She picked her way through the trees as quietly as she could, approaching the ship from a direction that wasn't easily visible from within. Reaching the ship wouldn't be hard. Getting up the ramp without Todd seeing her—that was the challenge.

She paused under the ramp and listened. Todd was still talking, taunting Adam. She let out a shaky breath. That meant Adam was still alive.

The ship was small and low to the ground. Evelyn could shimmy up onto the ramp at its midpoint, minimizing how long she'd be visible from inside. Branch in hand, she practically crawled on her belly till she could see into the ship.

Todd was focused on Adam. Even better, with her gone, Todd had moved so that he was standing near the ramp with his back to her. Evelyn had a clear shot.

She took a deep breath and held it, rising to her feet and noiselessly crossing the short distance between them. All the while, internally she chanted, *Please, please, please...*

When she brought the branch down on the back of Todd's head, hard enough that the wood made a loud cracking sound, she could barely believe it had worked. But Todd fell to the floor, the gun skittering out of his hand.

Evelyn kicked the silver disk out of Todd's other hand, then ran to get the gun. She shifted her club to her non-dominant hand, and wheeled around with the gun in the other.

"Take that, you... Oh," she said.

Adam was standing with the small silver disk held out toward Todd, who was still face-down on the floor. From the looks of things, Todd wasn't going anywhere any time soon.

The look on Adam's face was priceless. His eyes were wide, his mouth hanging open. He just kept staring at her.

Evelyn couldn't believe her plan had worked. She was

still shaking with adrenaline and felt like she might burst into tears or maniacal laughter at any moment. Or maybe throw up.

Instead, she pointed her branch at Todd and said, "Take that, asshat! Nobody messes with my planet or my man!"

A broad smile spread across Adam's face, though the wonder remained. "I will make sure everyone gets the message."

Chapter Twelve

Securing the liaison more permanently was a simple matter once Adam made a few adjustments to the suspension disk they commandeered. Figuring out what to do with him after was more troublesome.

Adam was just glad Todd couldn't talk while in stasis. Evelyn would probably hit him with her branch again. She'd kept it close by and was even talking about turning it into some sort of memento.

Thanks to her, the biggest problem Adam faced at the moment was dealing with her proximity and not being able to do anything about it. Once she had learned that his crew was on the way to take Todd into custody, she insisted that they not take their eyes off their prisoner, referencing half a dozen movies where the villain managed to slip away when the protagonists let down their guard.

Kissing Evelyn in front of Todd would just be awkward for everyone. Not that Adam really gave a damn what Todd thought.

Adam was saved when his second-in-command walked up the ramp.

"Khel," Adam said. "You arrived sooner than I anticipated."

They aligned their forearms and clasped each other's elbows in the customary greeting among the military ranks.

"The *Arbiter* is the fastest ship in the fleet," Khel said.

Two other crew members entered the skimmer and saluted Adam. He acknowledged the gesture with a nod.

Before coming to Earth, he would have dismissed them from his thoughts, trusting them to follow standard procedures without further interaction. Now, his attention lingered on the woman.

She was part of his crew, but they had never communicated through anything other than reports. Reports that he primarily ignored.

"Vay?" he said.

Her blue eyes widened and she tucked a lock of her short blonde hair behind her ear. It was a bit too long to meet regulations, but he let that pass.

"Yes, sir," she said.

He glanced at her companion, a hulk of a man who towered over her, his head and face devoid of hair. Ari— one of the highest ranked security officers from the *Arbiter*.

"Why did you bring the *Arbiter's* cultural programmer along on a security mission?" Adam said.

"I…" Vay clasped her hands in front of her, her cheeks turning pink as she held Adam's gaze. "I've been assisting with the research on Earth's…special situation." She glanced at Evelyn briefly before continuing. "And we didn't want to bring in too many people before you have a chance to review our report."

"General." Ari stood straighter, staring over Adam's shoulder. "Vay is fully trained in security protocols. By assigning her to this low-risk mission, she has an opportunity to observe a new planet while also assisting with the retrieval of the prisoner."

"I approved it," Khel said. "Vay makes an excellent point about the sensitivity of this matter. It seemed an efficient use of our resources."

"Very well." Adam handed the suspension disk to V-21-b3. Vay. "But your cultural observations will be extremely limited."

A bright smile spread across her face. "Even seeing Earth's ecosystem will give me invaluable insight into—"

Ari cleared his throat. Vay stopped speaking abruptly, resuming the placid expression she'd entered the ship with.

"Understood, sir," she said.

She put the suspension disk in a portable artificial gravity control unit and adjusted the settings till Todd's stasis field switched to anti-gravity. Todd floated into the air, enabling them to easily transport him to their ship.

"When you put him in the brig, make sure to turn off communications," Adam said.

He trusted his crew, but he didn't want Todd to even try to turn any of them. Besides, Todd was a jackass. Adam wanted to spare the guards from having to listen to him.

After Vay and Ari had left with the prisoner, Evelyn finally spoke up.

"That was way too gentle for my tastes. Couldn't they have knocked him down the ramp or something?"

"I'm just glad to be rid of him," Adam said.

Khel cleared his throat, then said, "You might not be rid of him, yet."

"Explain."

"You were right about this liaison. Not only was he smuggling contraband off of this planet, he was selling to some very important people. People with vast resources."

"Credits can't protect criminals from Coalition law. Contraband is illegal for a reason. Take this, for example." Adam handed Khel the gun they had taken from Todd.

"A projectile weapon?" Khel asked.

"That fires balls of metal using an explosive powder."

"That's barbaric." Khel shook his head as he examined the weapon. "The damage this would do to someone's flesh…"

"Exactly," Adam said.

"I suppose you guys use ray guns and just instantly disintegrate people in a civilized fashion." Evelyn flashed a brief, small smile.

Her shoulders were hunched and she was huddled against one of the walls as if she was trying to disappear into the paneling. The idea of her disappearing from his life terrified Adam more than the thought of the High Council itself seeking revenge on him after this.

He had watched enough of her sci-fi movies to understand what she was referencing with *ray guns.*

"As a matter fact, we do." Adam turned to Khel and said, "Forgive me, I haven't introduced you to the woman who saved me."

One eyebrow hitched up Khel's forehead. "That is a story I would like to hear."

Evelyn held up her branch. "Not much to tell. I just snuck up behind Todd and cracked this over the back of his head."

"A stick?" Khel said.

"A heavy stick." She wielded the branch with both hands as if it was a sword, swinging it through the air a few times. "I'm pretty good with wood."

She looked at Adam, a huge grin on her face. She didn't have to explain the joke for him to get it. He let out a loud laugh.

Adam didn't miss how Khel jumped at the sound. He had never heard Adam laugh before. Adam wasn't sure anyone outside of Earth had.

Evelyn grinned back at Adam. "So is it over? Can we finally get on with our lives?"

"I'll still need to put in the official request, but maybe Khel can help with that now."

"What request is that?" Khel asked.

"I'm staying. You will begin the procedure for me to relinquish my Coalition citizenship immediately."

Khel looked as if Adam had struck him. Rather than explain with words, Adam walked over to Evelyn's side and put his arm around her shoulders. Khel had the decency and good sense not to say anything, even though he gaped at them for a while.

"With all due respect," Khel said, "I don't think I've communicated how serious the situation is. Dozens of arrests have been made, but we don't yet know how high Todd Simms' connections reach. What we do know is that they all blame you for their current circumstances."

Adam had never given much thought to making enemies. He'd never had anything to lose—nothing that really mattered to him, anyway. Now, the thought of Evelyn in danger turned his blood to ice in his veins.

Khel's voice softened as he said, "You aren't safe here."

"If I leave, it won't fix anything." Adam was desperate for any reason, any excuse to justify staying. "Eventually, word will get out and they'll know that they can use her against me."

"Not if both your memories are wiped," Khel said. "She's not Coalition. She shouldn't know about any of this anyway."

Evelyn held up her hands, including the one holding the stick. "Hold on a minute. First of all, stop talking about me as if I'm not here and don't understand what you're talking about. Second of all, please explain exactly what you're talking about. I mean, I get the whole, *I'm in danger, he's in danger*, thing. But how much danger?"

Reality came crashing down on Adam. If he stayed on Earth as they had planned, he wouldn't have access to any technology. He wouldn't be able to protect either of them. At least if he returned to his command, he would be able to keep a ship in orbit. He could assign people he trusted to watch over her.

Quietly, he said, "Evelyn, if I stay here with you, we'll be dead inside of a month."

Her eyebrows lifted, but to her credit she didn't look afraid. "Okay, that's a lot of danger. How are we going to deal with it? And don't you dare talk about memory wipes. I don't like the sound of that at all."

Adam didn't either. Bad enough that Evelyn should forget him, but to forget her? The man he had become since he arrived on Earth would vanish. He didn't want to go back to who he was before. Still, he couldn't think of any other way.

"Khel, head back to the ship. One way or another, I'll send word soon."

Khel nodded before retreating down the ramp. Adam waited to speak until he was sure he and Evelyn were alone.

"I can't stand the thought of anything bad happening to you," he said.

"Can you stand the thought of anything bad happening to you? Because I'm about to hit you on the head with this stick. And I'm pretty good at it. Just ask Todd."

She wasn't laughing. A bad sign.

"There's no way that I can protect you," Adam said. "When they come for us—and they will—they'll kill us both. Or worse. You saw what Todd was able to do with a simple suspension disk. That's our equivalent of a zip tie. These people are corrupt. They will not respect the law. They'll come armed."

"So, have your buddies leave us some weapons. At least we'll have a fighting chance."

"I won't break the laws I've spent my life defending. Evelyn, I can't protect you. Not if I stay with you."

"Then take me with you."

Adam's blood started rushing through his ears. His mind filled with visions of a possible future with her.

Evelyn by his side on his ship. Evelyn safe behind the protection his rank and resources could afford them. Evelyn warming his bed every night and his heart every day. Evelyn far from her family, torn from her homeworld...

"You don't know what you'd be getting yourself into."

"I imagine it would involve whisking me away to a far off planet and traveling through space as a regular pastime." When Adam didn't deny it, she went on. "Do you even remember what my bedroom looks like?"

"My people are not what you're used to. You'd be

giving up so much to be with me."

"You were willing to give up even more to be with me. Besides, that's one of the benefits of not being genetically programmed for a specific role. I'm adaptable."

She had certainly proven that. Still, it seemed too good to be true.

"What about your family?" he said.

"We mostly talk through the Internet. I'm sure you can rig up a video call from Sadr-4. I'll make sure there isn't a view of space behind me. And if we do get a chance to visit around the holidays, you can get your fix of the great outdoors."

Could this actually work? Hope started to seep into his mind.

"They'll especially want us to visit when we start having children," he said, stepping closer to her.

Evelyn tilted her head back and laughed. "Oh, your doctors are going to love that. We might have the first one on Earth so someone from your crew can observe and learn."

"They'll probably faint."

"I would think your crew is made of sterner stuff."

His mind raced to meet this new challenge. There would be paperwork involved—there always was. Procedures to follow and protocol to fulfill. But having an Earthling join the Coalition was a much simpler process than what he would have faced to relinquish his own citizenship.

Having Evelyn at his side aboard the *Arbiter*, being able to keep her safe, to truly *be* with her… It was more than he could dream.

"I promise, we will make this work," he said.

"Well, there's one other promise you need to keep first. An implied promise, anyway."

He sifted through his memory, but couldn't figure out what she meant. Then she kissed him, and memories, thoughts, plans, all vaporized in the heat of just feeling her. When she pulled back, her smile was wicked. One eyebrow was raised expectantly.

Swallowing hard, Adam asked, "What promise is that?"

"Sex on a spaceship."

With a broad grin, he lifted her into the air. She wrapped her legs around his waist and laughed again.

"I am a man of my word."

Epilogue

K-58-b7 sat in her favorite window of listening station T5-Alpha, watching the changing patterns in the clouds covering Earth. The heavy feeling in her chest would not go away.

She shifted her gaze to the ship that was also orbiting Earth—that she could only see with the help of the nanites populating her brain. A faint shimmer along the edges of the massive ship's hull let her know its cloak was fully engaged.

The *Arbiter*, flagship of the Coalition of Planets. Commanded by General Serath himself, highest ranked military officer in the fleet.

"Why haven't they contacted me yet?" she murmured.

"Please restate inquiry." T5-Alpha's measured voice sounded over the station's intercom.

"Nothing." K-58-b7 shook her head. "Cancel inquiry."

She'd been alone too long. Talking to herself would only confuse the station's computer.

But talking to Brendan…

The tightness in her chest intensified. Any moment now,

the *Arbiter* would contact her. She would most likely be reassigned, since she'd already been alone on the station four times longer than she should have been. She would have to leave Earth. And him.

I wish I could at least say goodbye.

The base of her skull tingled, a silent inquiry from her nanites that switched her despair to panic.

"No, don't try to contact him."

If the nanites tried to initiate a connection with Brendan, the *Arbiter* would certainly detect it. He would likely be taken aboard and receive a mind-wipe, clearing all memory of their conversations.

She could bear the thought of never talking to him again much better than the thought of their relationship vanishing from his mind, as if it had never existed.

And if they looked more closely at her—and her nanites —at how she managed to contact him while bypassing T5-Alpha's controls and accessing the station's systems directly…

She shivered.

No, she wouldn't try to contact Brendan, even to say goodbye. She would wait for the *Arbiter* to contact her, and

—

Her thoughts cut off as the engines of the enormous vessel brightened. The aft thrusters fired, and before she knew it, the ship was just an afterimage on her retinas. It was gone.

Gone, and she was still there.

She should contact the ship, let them know that she'd been forgotten. But she had everything she needed to survive on the station. If she was reassigned again, she would be alone—just her and the malfunctioning robot friends in her mind.

At least stationed on Earth's listening station, she had *him*. She had Brendan.

Her heart pounded as she thought about the consequences of continuing their forbidden communication —and knew she would do it anyway. For as long as she could, as long as they had.

She shifted her gaze back to Earth, eager for his next transmission.

—

I hope you enjoyed *Gray Card!* The fun is just beginning with *The Department of Homeworld Security.* Read on for a sneak peek at K-58-b7's story. I'm sure she'd be fine with you calling her Kira.

Resident Alien

The Department of Homeworld Security
Book Two

Chapter One

"Greetings, my fellow interstellar travelers. This is Brendan Sloan, speaking to you from the little blue marble third from Sol. Without context, that doesn't give you much of a clue as to where I am, but if you're advanced enough to pick up this signal, I'm betting you can trace the source."

Brendan picked up the toy rocket that he kept on his desk and fidgeted with the stabilizers on its base. His stomach was full of butterflies—not the good kind—from his conversation with his sister, Paige.

She had been scheduled for a flight out of Louisiana earlier that day, but ran late at a cleanup site her environmental restoration team was working on. The plane had crashed. No survivors.

He felt terrible for the people who had been on board and for their families. And at the same time, he was grateful beyond measure that his baby sister had been spared. He was still having trouble wrapping his head—and his heart —around the situation.

"I'm keeping it short today, as I have something of a date." He hoped that Kira was listening. He needed to talk to her immediately—to hear her voice and know that she was okay as well. He spoke his mind, eager to finish the transmission.

"Humans have a need to bond. We bond with a partner, with our friends and family. With comrades-in-arms and comrades-in-ideas. It's part of what makes us strong as a species and something I hope our cultures will share. And if not, perhaps we can teach each other and grow through our own interactions."

He set the rocket down in front of a picture of him and Paige. He had his arms around her shoulders and was hugging her tight. Her expression was equal parts amused and annoyed.

They had the same blue eyes and red hair, same smile and scientific curiosity, but what they each added to the world was so different. She fought for the planet, hands on —often from the inside of a hazmat suit. Trying to get people to stop damaging their homeworld.

He worked with the government to create technology that was decades ahead of anything on Earth—tech that was supposed to be used to improve everyone's lives, but was usually turned into weapons to use against others. Hence his hiatus from his most recent project.

He ran his hands over his face, careful not to knock his headset out of place, then let out a sigh and leaned back in his chair.

"I look up at night and my eyes show me a sky filled with thousands of stars. My instruments let me know there are so many more out there, galaxies full of them in an infinite universe. And my reason tells me this—we cannot be alone. This is my official request to parlay. Please come in peace."

It was a silly dream and a waste of time—sending transmissions into deep space in the hopes that he might get lucky and reach an alien civilization, maybe hitch a ride and find a more peaceful home. But it kept him distracted from the problems on Earth and how very little he had been able to change anything. Yet.

Time and distance would help him come back to the communications project he was working on refreshed and with new perspective. Maybe he'd even figure out how to use their results to benefit all of humanity instead of only the people he worked for.

And thanks to taking time off, he had met Kira.

Officially, Brendan had been told that Eric was his

liaison. Eric checked in with Brendan once a month. Their conversations were superficial, but Brendan was sure Eric was under pressure from his superiors to get Brendan back on the project. Eric knew Brendan needed a break and more time to unwind. Brendan was pretty sure that was why they had assigned Kira to be a sort of handler for him. She talked to Brendan every day—pretending to be an alien.

His government sure was going the extra mile to help him recharge and get back on the job. He didn't want to admit how well it was working. If he knew he'd be working with Kira—that they might meet face-to-face—he'd ditch his lakeside cabin and head back to civilization in a heartbeat.

He wasn't sure when it had happened or how, but their talks had become the highlight of his day. He thought about her all the time. He even dreamed about her. Maybe today was the day he would tell her how he felt. After Paige's brush with death, he didn't want to risk never telling Kira the truth. Even if it made him feel like an idiot.

Falling for his handler was bad enough, but somehow he'd convinced himself that she felt the same way about him. He was probably going to make a royal fool of himself.

He flipped off his transmission, watching the power draw levels drop. Waiting—but never for long. He adjusted his headset and leaned forward.

"Brendan Sloan." Kira's voice flowed into his ears, rich

and deep and sexy as hell.

He closed his eyes and smiled before responding. "Kira I'm-too-mysterious-for-a-last-name."

A hint of laughter laced her words when she spoke again. "I thought today's broadcast was going to be about your theories on the best spots in the Sol system for setting up extra-terrestrial bases."

"I changed my mind."

"That's a shame. I'm looking to build a summer home."

He let out a laugh. Talking to Kira always made him feel...less alone in the universe.

"For you, only the best," he said. "Earth all the way."

"No bias there?"

"Come on. Try to stop and smell the roses on Jupiter, and you get a chest-full of ammonia crystals."

He was encouraged when she let out a little snort, so he continued.

"Then there's Mars," he said, "with its barely-there atmosphere and all those satellites taking pictures. How's anyone supposed to have any privacy? And robots running around on the surface, poking and prodding everything. I wouldn't want to live there."

"Right. Because once robots move in, there goes the neighborhood."

"They're up all hours whirring and running around. They pretend they're collecting samples, but you know they're just partying."

She laughed and it about did him in. He wanted to see the face that belonged to that steel-and-brandy voice. He could imagine her sitting across from him on the couch, leaning her elbow on the back of the cushions as they talked long into the night.

"Besides, you don't need to build a summer house in the Sol system—you're welcome in my cabin any time. There's no guest room, but it has a big bed."

He cringed the moment the words left his lips. *Smooth.*

Still, his mind leapt at the chance to add him to the scenario in a very carnal way. He shifted in his seat.

"And a very comfortable couch," he said. "Which is where I would be…in that event."

"It's a tempting offer, but I'm kind of stuck here."

"Right."

Wherever *here* happened to be. Probably a bunker outside of Bethesda.

He imagined her working in a sort of call center for handlers—everyone with headphones on, sitting in their cubicles and listening to their assigned assets while they shot rubber-bands at homemade dartboards.

"You sounded a little tense," she said.

"Picked up on that, did you?" Of course she did. Nothing seemed to slip past her notice.

"Do you want to talk about it?"

He shook his head, even though he knew she couldn't see him. "Just had a close call. Too close for comfort. It's made me think about not taking things for granted. Or letting opportunities pass."

She was silent, so he went on.

"Look, I know you're my handler."

"I have said no such thing."

"Right. I forgot. You're an alien." Because *that* was more likely.

"I've never confirmed that, either."

"Yeah, and you haven't denied it. When you first responded to my transmission, you wouldn't tell me how you picked it up and the only people capable of doing that are the ones in the group I work with."

"Or the advanced alien civilization you're trying to reach."

"There you go teasing me again."

"Sorry."

He could practically hear the smile in her words. It was contagious.

"I may just be a nerd to you—"

"You're not *just* anything to me," she said.

There was heat to her words. That was much worse than teasing him about being an alien. If she didn't care, why would she get so worked up? Why would she say something like that? He expected her to backpedal, but her tone was still serious when she went on.

"I wasn't supposed to talk to you," she said. "I'm just here to listen. But I couldn't...*not* respond. I had to talk to you, to get to know you. And I don't regret it. No matter what happens next, I'll never regret getting to know you."

His heart picked up. It sounded like she was saying goodbye.

"What's going on?"

"There have been some changes here," she said. "Big changes. I don't know when it will happen, but it's only a matter of time before I'm removed." Her voice cracked and she coughed as if she was clearing her throat.

His stomach felt like it had suddenly turned to lead. No daily talks with Kira to look forward to? No one to bounce ridiculous ideas off of and philosophize about society's ills and strengths?

The loneliness that had plagued him throughout his life started pushing back into his heart. He knew she had been lonely too, before they started talking. He could hear it in her voice. It was part of what bound them together. In all the world—in all the universe—they had found each other. He didn't want to lose her.

"I'm shocked they haven't already shut me down," she said.

His dread increased.

If she was anything like Eric, she'd been trained as a spy —received the full package. Brendan never let himself consider the baggage associated with being a handler. Sure, he considered that she might be using techniques to win his heart and seduce him into a course of action that might not be his own choice, like going back to work early. But hearing her talk about being *shut down* brought other aspects of her role to light. Ugly possibilities.

"Are you safe?"

"Yeah, just in deep trouble. But I don't care." Her voice was strong—almost harsh. But it softened as she went on. "Talking to you, getting to know you…has been the greatest experience of my life. I wouldn't trade it for anything."

"If your job was to convince me to come back, it worked. Tell them it worked. Tell them whatever they need to—"

"Hang on a second."

There was a pause when all he heard was the blood rushing through his ears.

"Something's wrong," she said. "I have to go."

"Kira, wait," he said. "I love you."

The signal died.

—

About the Author

USA Today Bestselling author Cassandra Chandler uses her vivid imagination to make the world more interesting, spawning the ideas she turns into her whimsical Science Fiction romcoms and darkly evocative Paranormal and Urban Fantasy Romances. Fast-paced and funny, lighthearted or dark, her stories will introduce you to characters you want to be friends with and worlds where you'd like to build a vacation home.